Palaces, Peasants a...
England in the 14th...

Written by Richard Platt

Illustrated by Robin Lawrie

Contents

Collins

The 14th century

The story of England in the 14th century is not one tale, but two. For England's kings and powerful barons, who owned much of the land and property, it was an exciting story of battles for power, wars against foreign foes and a pleasant life of **luxury** and plenty.

For ordinary poor people, the story was a very different one. In the 14th century, England was a country of green, rain-soaked fields and few towns. Those people who owned almost nothing lived in the countryside as peasants – poor farmers or farm workers. Ancient rules, laws and traditions controlled everything they did. Their lives were hungry, dirty, uncomfortable, exhausting and sometimes dangerous.

But before the century ended, these two stories came together in a violent struggle for power and freedom. When it finished, England had changed for ever.

Peasant life

In the 14th century, peasants survived by growing crops such as wheat, barley and oats and by raising a few animals to eat. They organised their lives around the changing seasons. They sowed their seed in the spring; they tended growing plants in the summer; and harvested them as autumn began.

Farm animals followed the same year-long cycle. New lambs and calves were born in the spring and fattened through the summer. There wasn't enough food to support all the animals through the winter, so many were killed around harvest time.

spring

summer

autumn

Food

Fourteenth-century English food was mostly **stodgy** and changed little from day to day. Peasants ate what their land and animals produced, plus whatever animals they could catch or trap. Their main crops were grains such as wheat and barley, plus peas or beans.

Bread was baked in an oven by a baker.

They ate the grains boiled up with water to make porridge, or baked into brown, heavy loaves. Mixing grain with yeast and water turned it into ale. Everyone drank this rich beer-like drink as a kind of liquid food. Even children drank a weak type of ale.

Peasants who were wealthy enough to own a cow or two had a supply of milk. From this they made cheese to add **variety** to their diet. Eggs from chickens made meals a little different, too.

When peasants ate meat, it was likely to be the very poorest kind because butchers sold the best meat to wealthy households. Peasants ate the animals' tails, fat, feet and heads – plus inside organs such as the liver and heart.

typical 14th-century food

leeks

onions

eggs

lamb's trotters

cheese

milk

sheep's heart

lambs' livers

sheep's head

Throughout the winter, those who could afford salted meat mixed it into their food to add flavour. Onions, garlic and herbs made food tastier. The other way to make meals more interesting was with fish and game (wild animals such as birds, rabbits and deer). However, all these animals were the property of the lord of the manor. Anyone caught fishing or hunting without permission faced a severe punishment.

In the 14th century there were no fridges or freezers, but could be preserved if it was dried out with salt or hung up in a smoky chimney.

Meat was smoked in a kitchen chimney.

7

Houses

Peasant families lived in houses built close together in small villages. Each house had a frame made of logs, roughly shaped with axes. Workers filled the spaces between these big timbers with rubble, or with a panel made of woven sticks smeared with mud and animal dung. Roofs were covered with thatch (a waterproof covering of straw or reeds). Glass was expensive, so windows were just draughty openings in the walls.

Inside the house there would have been just one room where the whole family lived, slept and ate together. They even shared the space with some of their animals. A dividing screen on one side kept the animals out of the living area.

The very poorest peasants lived in mud huts. Those who had a little more money would have lived in homes like this.

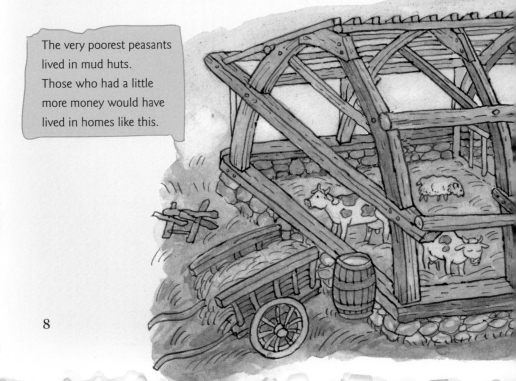

On cold winter nights the farm animals warmed the house: a cow produces as much heat as a modern electric fire. Most heat, though, came from a wood fire. Blazing in the middle of the room, it warmed the family and cooked their food. Bare earth, beaten hard by the family's feet, served as a floor.

Houses were bare: furniture was too expensive for poor families. To sleep, the whole family curled up round the fire – fully dressed – on simple mattresses made from sacks of straw or ferns. Bedtime came soon after sunset, because the only light came from the fire. Candles, made from **rushes** dipped in animal fat, were too precious for daily use.

Feudalism

The wealthy people who owned the land lived in castles and big houses, which stood at the centre of the large areas of land they owned, called manors. The peasants didn't own their houses, or the land they lived and worked on. It was owned by wealthy people and in exchange for their land and houses, peasants paid rent. Peasants not only paid rent with money, but also by doing jobs, such as growing crops for the landowner, or caring for his farm animals.

Peasants also had to pay the manor miller to grind their corn into flour and the manor baker to bake the flour into bread. The lord of the manor charged for countless other favours, such as hunting in the forest, or grazing animals among the trees. Even the dead couldn't escape these fees: when a peasant died, his lord would claim his best animal.

The great and wealthy men who owned the land also had the power to tell their peasants what they could and couldn't do. If the lord of the manor went away to war, men who worked on his land were expected to fight with him. This way of living was called feudalism. Poor people had to live and work in the place they were born, for the lord who owned their land, and they were not allowed to move away to work for someone else.

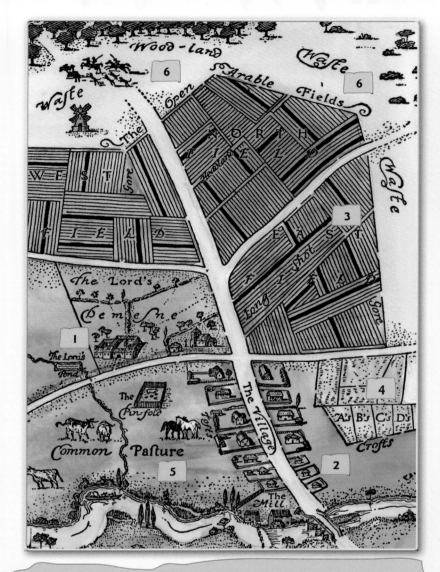

a 14th-century manor

1 the lord's manor house

2 peasants' houses

3 Land owned by the lord, and used by the peasants to grow crops such as barley. Each strip of land was farmed by a different family.

4 Land owned by the lord, and used by the peasants to grow vegetables.

5 Land owned by the lord, and used by the peasants to graze cattle.

6 Land owned by the lord, and used by the peasants to gather wood.

11

Childhood

Peasants' children also worked. In the 14th century, childhood didn't last as long as it does now as children became adults much earlier. Rich or poor, they were old enough to marry when they reached the age of 12. Above this age, if they did something wrong they were given exactly the same punishment as an adult.

Most poor people had an average of three children who survived to adulthood, but each new child meant more food had to be grown to feed them. Children had to help with this almost as soon as they could walk: even toddlers could scare away the birds that ate new green shoots. As they grew older, farm children could weed between the rows of crops, or clear stones from the soil. When they were teenagers, they worked alongside adults and learnt their jobs. There wasn't enough time or money for education and few poor people could read or write.

Children helped to weed between the crops.

Entertainment

Despite the peasants having to work so hard and being so poor, English villages were not boring, dismal places. Everyone knew how to enjoy themselves and took every chance to do so. People celebrated the coming of spring, the planting of crops, the middle of the summer and the harvest time. In mid-winter, they welcomed the return of the sun after the shortest day. Traditional festivals marked each of these events. Villagers dressed up to sing and dance and to carry out rituals. These were special actions that everyone learnt from their parents and then taught to their children. Today, the best known of these is the dance around the **maypole**.

Peasants danced around the maypole.

To accompany their dances, villagers didn't always need musicians. Their singing provided the tune and they kept time by clapping hands or beating out a rhythm. Where there were musical instruments, they were most likely to be a drum and a fife – a kind of whistle made from a bone or stick.

The Church also played a very important part in village celebrations. At Christian festivals such as Easter and Christmas there were special services, often with plays and performances.

Lord of the manor

A manor house was solidly built of brick and stone and often had several rooms spread over two floors. At the centre of the house, the family and their servants gathered to eat in the great hall. A big room, heated in winter by a blazing fire, the great hall would have had a large glass window to let in light.

Manor houses also had a private room where the lord and his family relaxed and slept on comfortable beds. At the other end of the hall, there were stairs leading up to guest bedrooms, with rooms for the storage and preparation of food and drink below. Because of the risk of fire, the kitchen was in a separate building.

Mealtimes in the manor house or castle were very different from in the peasants' homes. Wealthy people ate more meat and fish. Their cooks flavoured dishes with expensive spices brought by traders from the other side of the world. The lord of the manor washed down his **hearty** meals with wines brought over from France.

Plumbing in a 14th-century house looked very different! Toilets were flushed with rainwater collected from the roof, or with washing water.

a manor house

bedroom

great hall

kitchen

15

Education

In wealthy households, very small children were looked after by servants if their parents were busy. As they grew older, instead of working in the fields like peasant children, they studied. Schooling could begin when children were just four years old, but seven was more usual.

Any adult who knew how to read and write could teach a child to do the same and many children studied with their parents. They also learnt to read from servants, or monks, nuns and priests. The first things they learnt were their letters. Their teachers gave them alphabets pinned to wooden boards. Once they had learnt the letters, children studied a prayer book – not in English, but in Latin.

Latin was an ancient Italian language that was used in churches, in law courts and in government. Children neither spoke nor understood it, making learning to read very difficult. Only when they could read in Latin did children move on to English!

A few children studied in schools. For centuries, there had been song schools to teach the boys who sang in church and cathedral choirs. However, there were also a few schools in English towns that were not part of the Church. Most charged their pupils fees, but Grammar schools, which taught children for nothing, were beginning to appear.

Grammar schools were tiny, with just 20 or 30 pupils. They studied in a single room, with one master teaching children of all ages. Learning was a dull business: children memorised long pieces of writing, or grammar rules.

All the pupils at these schools were boys. Girls got little education, or none at all. Adults thought that learning was wasted on a woman. Her job was to be a good wife and for this she didn't need the kind of knowledge that came from books. For girls, education usually ended once they had learnt reading, writing and simple arithmetic.

Boys might grow up to do jobs that needed a lot of learning, so, for them, schooling continued. They learnt Latin and probably French as well. Very bright boys went on to study at a university. In the 14th century there were just two: Oxford and Cambridge.

University study wasn't as organised as it is today. There were no regular terms and students studied as and when they could. Those who stayed for four years earned a degree, as long as they could show how much they knew in an interview. Their teachers rarely set written exams and tests.

Learning to read and write made it possible for people to study almost any subject they chose – as long as they could find a book about it. This wasn't easy. Printing wasn't invented until the 15th century, so before that every book had to be copied out by hand, word by word. This made books extremely expensive. A typical book cost about 90p, at a time when a farm labourer earned only 1p a day.

In the 14th century books were carefully copied out by hand, like this.

The Church

Wealthy people were not the only ones with power in England. Christian leaders also commanded respect and obedience from the English people, rich and poor alike. The head of the Church was the Pope, who for most of the 14th century lived in France.

In England, archbishops and bishops were in charge of people's religion and the priests in churches and cathedrals. There were also monasteries and nunneries, where monks and nuns lived apart from the rest of the English people, praying many times each day. Abbots and priors controlled the monasteries.

Very religious people didn't just pray in church. Some became **pilgrims**, making religious journeys to visit holy places called shrines. There were shrines at Canterbury, Glastonbury and in several other towns. For most people, though, religion was about worship in a church or chapel. There, priests led services in Latin. For those who couldn't understand Latin, churches had coloured glass windows. Their pictures told stories in a kind of comic-book format.

People still go on pilgrimages today. One example is the *Hajj* that Muslims make to the holy city of Mecca in Saudi Arabia.

21

Tithes

In the 14th century religion was central to life. Everybody went to church to worship and to celebrate the Christian festivals.

The Church wasn't just important in leading religion. It was rich. Very rich. Most of the land not owned by the king or wealthy barons belonged to the monasteries and abbeys (great churches).

The Church also collected a tax from everybody called a 'tithe'. A tithe equalled one-tenth of everybody's property. If a hen laid ten eggs, for example, one of those eggs belonged to the Church. Altogether, the Church owned about one-third of England's wealth. Because of all this money, and because some of its leaders were dishonest and greedy, the Church wasn't very popular. For the peasants, it meant that they not only had to pay rent to the lord of the manor, but taxes to the Church, too.

Peasants paid their tithe to the Church.

Travel and transport

Although most poor people in the 14th century spent their entire lives very close to where they were born, and a day's journey to a market or a fair was a rare adventure, some poor people had to travel. Drovers, for example, had the job of moving geese, cows and sheep from farms where they were raised in Wales, Scotland and northern England to towns where people wanted to buy them for food. The journey from Wales to London was more than 500 kilometres and took three weeks.

For the wealthier, travelling was less unusual. Merchants made journeys to buy and sell everything from food to luxuries like expensive cloth and jewellery. Messengers brought news and letters. Skilled tradesmen travelled in search of work. Religious people made pilgrimages to holy places and rich barons made journeys between their homes in the town and country.

These travellers mostly rode on horseback. Horse transport was a luxury, because horses were expensive to buy. Horses were fussy about their food, too. They needed a special diet of oats. Travellers on horseback could cover 30–40 kilometres a day if they were lucky.

Vehicles were rare because roads were little more than tracks. Dusty in the summer, they were rutted, muddy swamps in the winter. In towns, the roads were sometimes good enough for horse-drawn carriages. But in the countryside vehicles with wheels often overturned or got stuck. Carts were reserved for very heavy loads that could not be carried in any other way.

Today, a journey of 30–40 kilometres would take about half an hour in a car.

For really long distances and for travel abroad, the sea was a speedy highway. Sailing ships could cover 11 kilometres in an hour. They could cross the English Channel between France and England in an afternoon in good weather.

Unfortunately, the weather – and the ocean tides – didn't always help the traveller. If the wind was blowing the wrong way, a ship could be stuck in port for weeks. Twice a day, low tides emptied the water from harbours, leaving ships caught in mud. Even if a ship sailed from the harbour, a storm could easily wreck it and drown the passengers. Many travellers visited churches to offer prayers and gifts to God before setting sail.

Today ocean travel is much safer and ships are much bigger. Eight 14th-century sailing ships would fit end-to-end on the deck of a modern Channel ferry.

Law and order

Travellers faced many other dangers besides shipwrecks.
Robbery and violence were perhaps the greatest of these.
Fourteenth-century England could be a rough and dangerous place.
There were laws to protect people against violence and stealing,
but no way to make sure that these laws were obeyed.

There was no police force to chase and capture criminals. Instead,
villagers were expected to police themselves. When anyone saw
a crime taking place, they had to shout to others to help them.
The crowd would then have to chase and capture the criminal.

Those who broke the law and got caught faced harsh punishments.
The penalty for stealing anything worth more than a shilling (about
two weeks' wages) was execution. Murder and
some other violent crimes were punished
in the same way.

If you were in the stocks,
your feet were put through
the holes and you were
locked in.

The punishment for lesser crimes could be branding – burning a mark on the skin – or the shame of the stocks and pillory. These were wooden frames set up in a market place to hold the hands or feet. Locked into them, a criminal had to put up with insults – or rotting vegetables – hurled by anyone passing.

These punishments did little to stop crime, and violence was very common. The risk of being murdered, for example, was possibly ten times greater than today.

Towns and trade

Though most of England's people lived in the countryside, towns and those who lived in them were important to the life and wealth of the country.

There were very few large towns. London was by far the biggest, with eighty thousand to one hundred thousand people living there. This is small compared to today, when nearly eight million people live and work in London.

Most towns were more like what we would call a village today. They were small enough for the citizens to tend their fields outside the town and to drive their animals into the town square to sell them on market day.

Towns were important because they were centres for making, buying and selling things. In their workshops, craftsmen shaped goods made of iron, wood and pottery. Masons carved stone into fantastic shapes to decorate fine buildings. Stinking tanneries turned animal skins into leather. Busy with their needles, tailors sewed fashionable clothes.

Today, few Londoners still make things. Just three in every hundred people work in factories and workshops.

The greatest of all industries was cloth-making and England became famous for its wool fabric. Town workers spun the wool into **yarn**. Weavers turned the thread into long rolls of cloth. Dyers gave the cloth a range of brilliant colours.

Cloth was dyed in a range of colours.

Almost all the work was done by hand. The only machines were in the metal workshops, called forges. There, huge water-powered hammers helped to beat out red-hot iron.

Town workers were careful to protect their valuable skills. They organised themselves into guilds – clubs with members from just one trade. Joining a guild wasn't easy. Craftsmen first worked as trainees, called apprentices, for at least five years. When they had learnt their skills, apprentices became "masters" and could work freely at their trades. They could also employ apprentices themselves. Craft guilds made sure that only apprentices or masters could work in their trade.

Tailors were also in a guild. A tailor is shown measuring cloth.

England still has guilds, but not just for crafts any more. Among the newest is the Worshipful Company of Tax Advisers!

Besides the workshops of the tradesmen, towns were crowded with other buildings. Many of them were houses. The finest were built several storeys high, with solid stone walls. They had glass in the windows and their woodwork was elegantly carved and painted. These grand and expensive homes showed off the wealth and importance of their owners.

Poorer people lived in smaller, more humble wooden houses like those in villages.

The town's poorest people crowded together in cramped, smelly **slums**. Their dark, small homes were filthy and airless. Whole families lived together in a single room.

a wealthy family's house

One London street had eight shops in just 21 metres.

Markets and shops were also part of the town scene. On a market day traders put up their stalls in the town's largest open space. Market squares were also used for selling animals. On one day of the week they were filled with a bleating, mooing, grunting, honking mass of fur and feathers.

Shops existed only in the biggest towns. They were very simple, often being just the front room of a house with windows open to the street. They were also very small. Shops sold all sorts of goods that people could not make themselves: everything from knives and leather goods to cloth, armour, medicines and shoes.

Living and working in towns was unhealthy, noisy, smelly and risky. Few of the services that we are used to today existed then. No street lighting meant that the towns were very dark at night, with criminals often lurking in the shadows.

Fresh water flowed from wells in the street and from taps only in finer houses, but there were no proper sewers. Human waste had to be carried away in carts. Sometimes it overflowed across the streets in stinking pools.

Rats and dogs ran everywhere. They fed on the rubbish that butchers and other tradesmen threw from their shops. Live animals roamed freely in the streets and dead ones lay for days where they fell, as it was nobody's job to pick them up. Even the air was foul. In earlier times, city dwellers used wood and charcoal for heating and cooking. Now coal burned in more and more hearths and stoves, giving off a foul smoke that clouded the air.

One of the reasons for the crowded state of cities was that walls enclosed them. Built centuries earlier to protect towns from foreign invaders, walls remained long after the threat of attack had gone. They stopped the city growing and spreading out. As the **population** got bigger, more and more people lived within the same small space.

Town streets were not paved, so rain turned them into muddy swamps. Even today outside some very old city buildings you can still see the scrapers people used to remove street mud from their shoes.

Warring kings

Edward I

Towns in the 14th century may not have needed their walled defences, but for most of the 13th century England had been at war. At that time, the most powerful man in England was the king. King Edward I, known as Edward Longshanks, was aged 69 at the start of the 14th century. Old and tired, in his 28 years as king, Edward had led his army into battle many times.

Edward I

In Scotland, he battled **clans** who hated English rule, and he fought and defeated the Welsh, who loathed English rule as much as the Scots did. After crushing the last rebellion in Wales, Edward I built a whole chain of castles to show off his power. He even gave his son the title 'Prince of Wales', which is still used today.

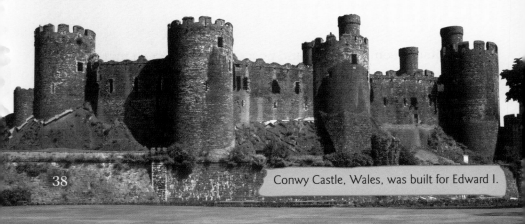

Conwy Castle, Wales, was built for Edward I.

Edward I fought battles in Wales and Scotland.

The king had been in trouble in France, too. England ruled Gascony in south-west France and he sent an army there when the French king, Philip the Fair, tried to conquer and rule the region. To make peace, Edward married Philip's sister Margaret in 1299. However, it was a marriage for power, not love. Edward still missed his beloved first wife Eleanor of Castile, who had died ten years before.

England itself seemed settled and peaceful. Most agreed that the king ruled wisely and fairly. His people respected him as a godly and just man. But they also feared him. He was very tall (his nickname, Longshanks, meant "long-legs"), with a fiery temper.

Although King Edward I was powerful, even he could not always do exactly what he wanted. At that time, the king shared power with the country's noblemen and religious leaders. Working with them wasn't easy and the result was often an uncomfortable and bad-tempered partnership.

King Edward I in parliament.

The noblemen were the heads of wealthy and powerful families and the king depended on their help and support. They gave him the money he needed to run the country and in times of war they also supplied the king with an army of **knights**. King Edward also had no choice but to take the advice of members of the Church – archbishops, bishops and abbots – because of their power and wealth.

Today, neither the **monarch** nor the Church has the power to make laws. Members of Parliament are elected by the people, rather than being chosen because of how much money they have.

When the king needed help, or wanted to raise money in taxes, he brought together the nobles and clergy in a parliament. Since the century before, parliaments also included the heads of other wealthy families chosen by the people of the towns and counties. Together, parliament and the king made laws and ruled England.

Edward clashed with parliament when he raised taxes to pay his troops. The wars in Scotland, Wales and France cost a lot of money and the clergy and noblemen didn't want to pay more.

Edward was still battling with parliament – and with the Scots – when his reign as king of England ended with his death in 1307. While crossing the Scottish **border** to end another rebellion – led by Robert the Bruce, the King of Scots – Edward died of a gut infection.

Edward II

On his father's death, Edward II became king. The two men couldn't have been more different. Edward I was a serious man who earned the country's respect as a strong but fair king. His son didn't have the same **authority** and people thought him weak. He spent money freely and he preferred music and play-acting to fighting wars.

Edward II

King Edward II continued his father's **campaigns** against the Scots, but with much less success. The power of Robert the Bruce grew partly because of the way he fought. He avoided spreading out his men to face the English enemy in a large battle. Instead, his soldiers used surprise attacks, killing their foes quickly, before escaping to the wild bogs and moors. These battle skills helped him to take control of most of Scotland.

Robert the Bruce

The king wanted to stop Robert the Bruce capturing the whole country, so in June 1314 he marched his entire army north. At the Battle of Bannockburn that followed, the English soldiers faced half as many Scots. Edward was sure that his stronger army would win, but he was wrong. Strong, brave Scots spearmen fought so hard that the English soldiers panicked. They were exhausted by fighting on swampy ground and as many as two-thirds of the English army died in a bloody defeat.

The Scots were not Edward's only problem. The barons, powerful English noblemen, wanted to get rid of Edward's closest friend, the Earl of Cornwall, Piers Gaveston. They felt that the king liked him too much and they felt he had too much power over Edward. The barons forced Edward to **banish** Gaveston to Ireland in 1308. When Gaveston returned, the barons rebelled against the king and his favourite. They captured Gaveston and killed him.

Edward continued to **tussle** for power with the barons. They rebelled again when the King formed another very close friendship with a young nobleman called Hugh le Despenser.

This time the king was victorious, but his triumph didn't last long. His wife Isabella, daughter of the King of France, became jealous of Despenser. She left Edward – and England – and returned home to France. In France, she fell in love with an English nobleman, Roger Mortimer, and together they raised an army and invaded England.

Queen Isabella returned home to France.

Queen Isabella and Roger Mortimer raised an army against Edward II.

Because he was deeply unpopular, Edward could do nothing about the invasion since nobody would join his army. Parliament took him prisoner and forced him to abdicate – give up the right to be king. His son (also called Edward) was crowned king in his place at the start of February 1327.

Edward II lived on until October, when he was murdered, probably by men working for Isabella and Mortimer.

Edward III

Edward III was just a boy of 14 when he became king, but he spent the next 50 years putting right his father's mistakes. He regained the support of the barons and, with their help, money and soldiers he fought successful wars against the Scots and the French.

Edward III in later life

When a group of powerful Englishmen lost lands in Scotland, they organised a private invasion to try to regain them. When this scheme went wrong, Edward sent his own troops and in 1333 recaptured much of southern Scotland. However, the Scots fought back, forcing Edward to arrange a **truce**.

The Scots were able to strike a bargain because of their powerful **ally**: France. Edward didn't dare to make outright war on Scotland, because he feared the French would join the war and, together, the two countries could defeat England. However, in the end the truce only delayed the war. When it began in 1337, Edward could not have guessed how serious the fight with France would be.

Edward III signed a truce with the Scots.

The Hundred Years War

The war with France started – and continued – for several reasons. England had for a long time ruled parts of what is today called France. However, the kings of the two countries could never agree where the border should be. They also argued about the rights of each other to buy and sell wool, which was important to both countries. Scotland was a problem, too: both England and France claimed the country as their own.

The biggest prize, though, was the crown of the French king. The English kings believed that they should wear it and rule France because some of their ancestors had married French royalty and this gave them a claim to the French throne.

Gascony was ruled by England.

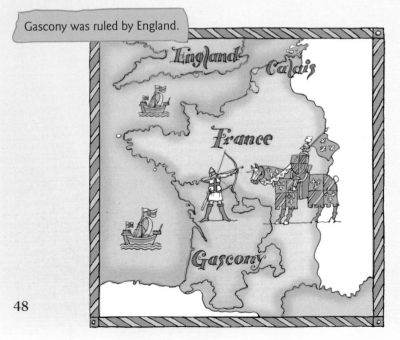

War began in 1337 when the French king claimed Gascony, a region of south-west France under English control. Edward III hit back by invading the north of the country, aiming to conquer and rule all of it.

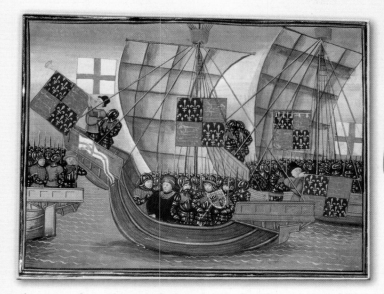

Edward III's troops sailed to France.

The French and English fought each other until 1453. At times, England came close to winning, such as the time when Edward's armies won a great victory at the Battle of Poitiers in 1356 and captured the French king.

But despite this and other victories, as well as spending huge sums of money on soldiers and sailors, England could not defeat the French. When the war finally ended, the English king *still* didn't rule France, apart from one tiny part: the town of Calais, on the English Channel. Today it's a famous ferry port.

Fighting in France didn't continue all the time, but the Hundred Years War came to be the most important event in Edward III's reign. It was very expensive and it also made it more difficult for him to **govern** England. He could not be both in London and leading his soldiers on the battlefield in France.

The war also had disastrous effects on the people of both countries. In England, its cost led to high taxes. Fought mostly in France, the war caused chaos and destruction there, too. Huge numbers of soldiers hacked at each other with **crude** weapons, in a muddy, confused and desperate struggle. When they were not fighting, the soldiers roamed the countryside. They **plundered** food from farmers and stole anything of value.

English and French soldiers fought each other in France. Many people died in battle during the Hundred Years War.

Though the war was terrible for the peasants of France and England, it changed forever the way armies fought each other. England won significant battles in France by the skilful use of longbows. Using them, English archers could fire a dozen arrows in a minute, so that they fell on the enemy literally like deadly rain. French archers used crossbows, which were six times slower.

a crossbow

English longbows were better than the French crossbows in battle.

The two countries also fought with a completely new weapon:
the cannon. The very first cannons, used from around 1326,
produced a lot of smoke and noise, but did little damage.
However, by the end of the war cannons were very destructive.
They could punch holes in the thickest walls, so that castles were
no longer safe places. The army of the French king, Charles VII,
used their cannons to capture almost 60 fortresses and walled cities
in Normandy, north-west France, in less than a year.

The Hundred Years War would kill many Englishmen on the battlefields of France, but far more died at home of hunger and disease. In 1315, torrential rain soaked Europe, destroying crops. It became hard to find food and, when it was available, no one had enough money to buy it. The price of wheat, which people needed to make bread, was eight times higher than normal. Eventually, farmers were forced to eat the seed corn they had saved from the harvest for planting the following season. Though this kept them alive a little longer, it meant that they could grow no more crops, as they had no seed to sow.

Desperate with hunger, people ate grass, the bark from trees, or human flesh. The hungriest people dug up graves to eat the bodies of people who had just been buried.

The shortage of food did not just affect the poor. Even England's king, Edward II, sometimes went hungry. When he visited St Albans in August there was no bread in the town to feed him or anyone travelling with him.

The terrible weather continued for three years and starvation and illness killed up to a quarter of Europe's population. Food supplies did not return to normal until ten years after the famine began.

The Black Death

In the middle of the century an even worse natural disaster struck England. A dreadful disease nicknamed the "Black Death" spread through the country. Anyone who caught it suffered a high fever. Then a huge blister called a bubo appeared, turning the skin black. Most people died in a couple of days.

The disease first appeared in England in a Dorset port in June 1348. A sailor infected with the Black Death came ashore and died soon after. By autumn, the disease had reached London. It spread through the whole country the following summer.

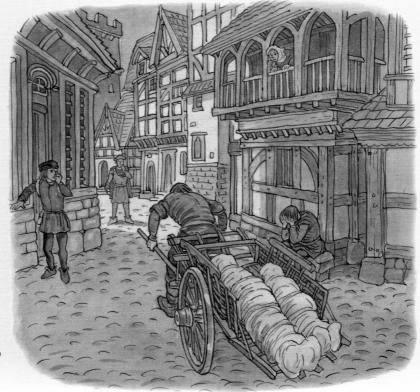

People who had the Black Death went to ask their priest for help.

The Black Death was frightening because it killed so quickly, because it killed so many people and because nobody knew the cause. People blamed hot baths, luxury living, fruit and even tight clothing. Priests urged people to avoid sin (wicked or rude behaviour) and told them that prayer would protect them. It didn't. Even those who prayed the hardest died. Doctors were no more help. They sold useless herbal remedies, or opened people's veins to let the blood run out. Nothing worked.

Today, it's thought that the Black Death was a disease called bubonic plague. It's spread by the fleas that live on rats. When the rats die, the fleas hop on to humans. The fleas' bites pass on the disease.

Because poor people in England's towns lived in cramped, dirty houses where fleas and rats **thrived**, it was there that the Black Death spread quickest. Wealthy people thought they could escape the danger. They fled from London to their country homes where there were fewer people – but they carried the disease with them.

Though the plague spread more slowly in the countryside, it still killed many people. Crops rotted in the fields because there was nobody to harvest them. Dead bodies weren't buried because people were too ill to dig graves. Whole villages were deserted because when so many people died, the rest ran away to other villages.

The Black Death spread quickest in warm weather and when the summer of 1349 ended, so too did the disease. In England, it killed over one and a half million people – between a third and half of the population.

The Black Death came at a time when the English way of life started to change slowly. For centuries, peasants paid for their land and homes not with money, but by working for their masters. Now this system of feudalism was gradually ending: peasants began selling their produce and paying rent in money for their land. Workers with no land received wages in coins.

The bonds that tied people to the land were getting less strong, too. Freed from old laws that ruled their lives, workers could move away from the villages where they had been born. They could travel to places where a new master would pay them better.

The old ways of doing things didn't change instantly. Even where money replaced traditional duties, masters often still expected to have comfortable, pleasant lives. Poor people hated the old-fashioned feudal ways and the tithes of the Church. They envied their wealthy masters and wanted more freedom.

The Black Death made the changes come faster. Those who survived the terrible disease found that they had new power. They could charge much more for their work. Fit, young, strong men were hard to find. Wealthy people who needed work done now were asked to pay much more. Builders' wages, for example, roughly doubled.

The people who owned England's land and property hated paying the higher wages. In parliament, the rich demanded that working people must stop charging so much. King Edward III agreed and parliament passed two laws to force people to work and cutting their pay. These laws angered many poor people, but it wasn't Edward III who faced their fury.

In autumn 1376 the king fell ill. Edward III's eldest son had died in the summer of 1376, so when the king died in 1377, his ten-year-old grandson became king: Richard II. As he was too young to govern England, Richard's uncle, John of Gaunt, ruled for him.

John of Gaunt

The Peasants' Revolt

The laws on wages that Edward III had agreed to did little to keep pay down. Workers still demanded – and got – more money than before for each day's work. But the new laws had an effect that parliament didn't expect. They made England's working people distrust their masters. Workers saw the laws as an unfair punishment for simply wanting a better life.

The laws didn't just limit wages. They also required everyone to work for nothing for their masters – the barons and lords who still owned much of the land – before they did any work for wages. It was a return to the ways of the past which poor people hated.

Anger grew when workers were punished for daring to ask for higher pay. And it rose into fury after the king brought in new taxes, to pay for the costly wars in France. All adults were forced to pay these new taxes – the 1381 tax was a shilling, about two weeks' wages.

In May 1381, the angry workers rebelled. Villagers in Essex refused to pay the tax. They attacked an official sent to round up and punish **tax-dodgers**. As news of the rebellion spread, people all over Kent and Essex joined in, leaving their homes to march on London.

Among the leaders of the rebels were Wat Tyler, John Ball and Johanna Ferrour. Wat Tyler was a builder and he led Kentish rebels to Canterbury, then on to London. Preacher John Ball had been in trouble for his fiery sermons. He believed that all men and women were equal, but this was a dangerous message. It threatened England's noblemen, who expected less wealthy people to work for them and obey their orders.

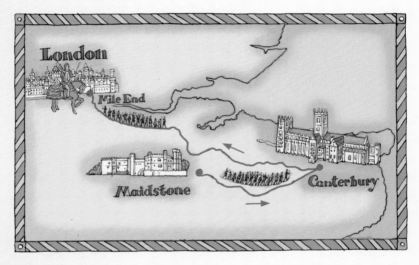

The rebels reached London on 13 June 1381. On their way, they opened jails to release the prisoners. They attacked government buildings and the estates of some of the country's wealthy rulers. Johanna Ferrour set fire to the Savoy, the grand home of Richard II's uncle, John of Gaunt. The following day she led a **mob** to the Tower of London. They dragged out the Archbishop of Canterbury and another official and beheaded them.

Rebels attacked the Tower of London.

The rebellion gathered so much force that it now threatened the power of parliament and of the boy king, Richard II. Richard, only 14 years old, met a group of rebels at London's Mile End. There, he agreed to many of their demands. He promised to lower land rents and to release from prison those who refused to pay the new tax. The next day, he met Wat Tyler and the rebels from Kent. They gathered at Smithfield, a large field where farm animals were bought and sold, just outside of London's walls.

Wat Tyler made many of the same demands that the rebels had made the day before.

The left side of the picture shows Wat Tyler being stabbed to death in front of Richard II. The right side of the picture shows Richard II addressing the mob.

Again, the king agreed to them and told Tyler to go home. However, the rebel leader didn't trust the king, whose supporters were angry and insulting. Suddenly, one of the king's supporters, the Mayor of London, pulled out a sword and stabbed Wat Tyler in full view of the rebel crowd. The rebels rushed forwards with a bloodthirsty cry.

Surrounded, the king could not escape. He calmly turned his horse and rode to meet the rebel mob. "Sirs, will you shoot your king?" he said. "I am your captain, follow me." He walked his horse slowly away and the astonished rebels followed him. The king told them he would forgive them if they returned to their homes. And so, brilliantly and bravely, he ended the revolt.

Richard II's bold action at Smithfield ended the greatest threat to royal rule that England had ever seen. It earned him the respect of the English people. However, the king didn't keep his word. He rounded up the leaders of the revolt and executed them. Then he broke the promises he had made to the rebels.

Richard II dealt with the leaders of the revolt skilfully and ruthlessly, but he had less luck in handling the noblemen who paid the country's bills.

When John of Gaunt visited Spain in 1386, the Earl of Gloucester and his allies plotted to take control of the government and they banished or killed Richard's friends and supporters. Richard managed to regain his power and for eight years he allowed his rivals to rule with him. But in 1397, he got his revenge on the plotters. He ordered the Earl of Gloucester and some of the others to be murdered. The rest he banished abroad or threw in prison.

It was a dangerous move and two years later Richard took another risky decision. When John of Gaunt died, Richard took all his uncle's lands and wealth and banished John's son, Henry Bolingbroke, forever. This enraged Henry, who wanted to regain his father's property. While Richard was in Ireland trying to stop a revolt against English rule, Henry invaded England.

When Richard returned from Ireland in August, he realised he didn't have the support to fight Henry's army and could no longer rule. He abdicated and was thrown in prison. His cousin Henry Bolingbroke became King Henry IV in the last autumn of the century. Richard starved to death in prison a few months later.

Henry Bolingbroke was crowned King Henry IV of England.

The end of the century

When the 14th century ended, England was very different from how it had been in 1300.

By joining together, England's peasants realised that they could start to change things they didn't like and they were much freer than they had been a century earlier. The Peasants' Revolt may not have achieved everything that its leaders planned, but it helped to end the feudal system, with its ancient rules, rights and duties.

14th-century silver coins

The rich barons of England held on to their money and their land, but they had learnt that there were limits to their power. They could no longer expect automatic obedience from the poor peasants on their land. Nor could they force them to work for nothing, or for low wages.

The revolt changed the scene for the king, too. He didn't dare to impose extra taxes. Nor did the kings and queens who followed him. The country would never be quite the same again.

sheep-**shearing**

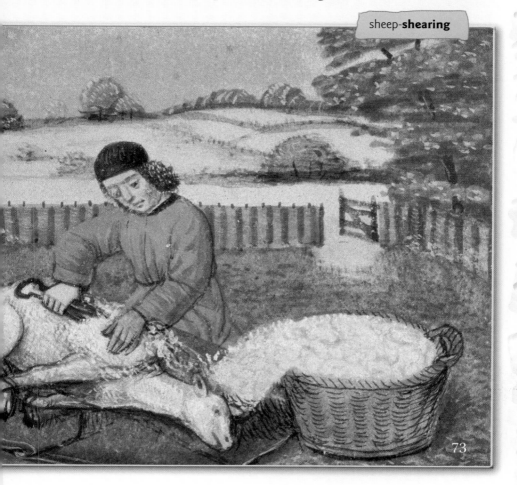

73

Glossary

ally	a friend or supporter, especially in war
authority	the ability to get others to agree with and obey you
banish	send someone away
border	the boundary between two countries
campaigns	stages in a war, spent finding and fighting an enemy
clans	family groups
crude	simple or basic
govern	to rule or control
hearty	nutritious and plentiful
knights	soldiers who rode horses and wore armour
luxury	something that you don't need, but that makes life more comfortable
maypole	a pole around which people dance on May Day holding long ribbons
mob	a group of angry, violent people
monarch	king or queen

pilgrims	religious people who travel to worship at a holy place
plundered	used violence to take someone's property
population	the people of a place
rushes	large grass-like plants that grow on wet soil
shearing	removing a sheep's wool using clippers
slums	houses that are not fit to live in
stodgy	heavy, dull and filling
tax-dodgers	people who don't pay their taxes
thrived	did well
truce	an agreement to stop fighting
tussle	to argue or fight
variety	difference, choice or change
yarn	thread used to make cloth

Index

A century of change

Edward I	Edward II	Edward III
Ruled 1272–1307	Ruled 1307–1327	Ruled 1327–1377
Fought wars with Wales, Scotland and France	Defeat at Bannockburn 1314	Truce with Scotland. The Hundred Years War with France started 1337
Feudal system: peasants worked for the landowner	Famine 1315–17	The Black Death killed half a million people in England in 1348–49

Richard II Ruled 1377–1399 	Henry IV Ruled 1399–1413 
Richard put down the Irish in 1399 The Hundred Years War with France continued 	Henry Bolingbroke invaded England 1399 The Hundred Years War with France continued 
The Peasants' Revolt 1381 	End of the feudal system 

Ideas for reading

Written by Clare Dowdall, PhD
Lecturer and Primary Literacy Consultant

Reading objectives:
- summarise the main ideas drawn from more than one paragraph, identify key details that support the main ideas; retrieve, record and present information from non-fiction
- read books that are structured in different ways
- explain and discuss their understanding of what they have read, including through formal presentations and debates

Spoken language objectives:
- participate in discussions, presentations, performances, role play, improvisations and debates
- use relevant strategies to build their vocabulary
- give well-structured descriptions, explanations and narratives for different purposes
- maintain attention and participate actively in collaborative conversations
- articulate and justify answers, arguments and opinions

Curriculum links: History

Interest words: ally, bubonic plague, campaigns, clans, feudalism, guilds, monarch, pilgrim, tithes, truce

Resources: whiteboard, space for freeze frames, ICT

Build a context for reading

This book can be read over two or more reading sessions.

- Read the title and blurb. Check that children know exactly what a century is and when the 14th century was, i.e. 1300–1399.
- Ask children to look for new or challenging words in the title and blurb. Discuss what *famine*, *plague* and *revolution* are and ask children if they can think of any examples from recent times to build a context for their reading.

Understand and apply reading strategies

- Read the text on p2 aloud. Ask children to notice how this historical account is being organised, e.g. it is two stories that will meet with some sort of battle at the end that brings the stories together.
- Ask children to read to p14, noting what it was like to be a peasant in the 14th century. Ask each child to feed back on one aspect that they have read about, e.g. food, feudalism and together, construct a spider-diagram containing important facts about peasant life.